REST IN PEACE RASHAWN RELOADED

WRITTEN BY: RONNIE SIDNEY, II, LCSW

ILLUSTRATED BY : TRACI VAN WAGONER

Rest in Peace RaShawn Reloaded

Published by Creative Medicine: Healing Through Words, PO Box 2749, Tappahannock, VA, 22560

Library of Congress Control Number: 2017901390
ISBN 978-978-099-001-5 (Hardback)
ISBN: 978-978-099-002-2 (Paperback)
ISBN 978-978-099-000-8 (Paperback)

PRINTED IN THE USA

Rest in Peace RaShawn Reloaded
Written by: Ronnie Sidney, II, LCSW
Illustrated by: Traci Van Wagoner
Designed by: Kurt Keller
Edited by: Tiffany Carey Day, Francesca Lyn and Samantha Willis
Contributor: Laurence Jones

Please visit www.nelsonbeatstheodds.com for information about "Rest in Peace RaShawn Reloaded", "Nelson Beats the Odds", "Tameka's New Dress", and "Nelson Beats the Odds Compendium One". The "Nelson Beats the Odds Comic Creator" app, teacher's guide and mixtape are also available on the website. Follow us on social media and use the hashtag #RipRashawn #TamekasNewDress, #NelsonBeatsTheOdds, #NBTO and #iBeatTheOdds.

 @nelsonbeatstheo

 @nelsonbeatstheo   @ronniesidneyii

 Nelson Beats The Odds
Ronnie Sidney, II, LCSW
#iBeatTheOdds

 @nelsonbeatstheo   @ronniesidneyii

Creative Medicine: Healing Through Words, LLC

FOREWORD

Our young people are being traumatized daily by directly experiencing violence, or viewing violent videos of men, women, and children being killed by private citizens or police officers. My hope is that "Rest in Peace RaShawn Reloaded" gives young people a platform to process police-involved shootings, gangs, and grief. As adults, it's essential that we're physically and emotionally available to help our young people through these processes.

The JMU Male Academy for Academic Achievement invited me to speak on July 18, 2016. The event was in the wake of the officer-involved shootings in St. Paul, Baton Rouge, and Dallas. I deviated from my initial presentation because I knew the recent shootings were on everyone's minds. I divided the young men into groups of six and asked them to answer the following questions: What solutions do you think will bridge the divide between communities of color and the criminal justice system? What are your opinions on the recent officer-involved shootings? What is it like to be Black or Hispanic today? The questions and answers give a real voice to a fictional story, and are presented throughout "Rest in Peace RaShawn Reloaded".

The National Football League (NFL) protests, led by Colin Kaepernick, inspired the "Rest in Peace RaShawn Reloaded" cover. The cover also honors the courage of Eric Reid, Seth DeValve, and Michael Bennett. Those four men, along with many others, took a peaceful stand against social injustice and oppression. The NFL players cannot do it alone, it will take ALL of us coming together as ONE to end police brutality and community violence #ImWithKap

Second Print 2017

JEREMY WAS TIRED OF BEING PICKED ON BY LIL' G AND THE SAUCE STREET GANG SO HE ASKS HIS MOTHER TO TAKE HIM TO SHOPPERS WORLD.

JEREMY WALKS AROUND THE STORE LOOKING FOR SOMEONE OVER THE AGE OF 18 TO BUY HIM AN AIRSOFT GUN.

THANKS, HERE IS THE MONEY I OWE YOU.

HEY, COULD YOU BUY THIS FOR ME? I'LL GIVE YOU AN EXTRA $20.

"Airsoft guns are replica firearms that shoot plastic pellets (also known as BBs) by way of compressed gas or electric and/or spring-driven pistons. Depending on the mechanism propelling the pellet, an airsoft gun can be operated manually or cycled by either compressed gas such as Green Gas (propane and silicone mix) or CO2, or by compressed air via a spring or an electric motor pulling a piston. All these products are designed to be non-lethal and to provide realistic replicas" (Nedivi, 2012).

HABIB, A LOCAL STORE OWNER, WATCHES JEREMY WAVE HIS AIRSOFT GUN AND CALLS 911.

RASHAWN GOES TO GET NELSON AND JEREMY FROM THE PARK BEFORE THE STREET LIGHTS CUT ON.

JEREMY ANXIOUSLY PUTS THE AIRSOFT GUN UNDERNEATH HIS HOODIE.

RASHAWN SEES A BIG BULGE IN JEREMY'S HOODIE AND ASKS...
WHAT'S UNDERNEATH YOUR HOODIE?
WHAT ARE YOU, CRAZY? WHERE DID YOU GET IT FROM?
MOM BOUGHT IT FOR ME.

"What solutions do you think will bridge the divide between communities of color and the criminal justice system?"

"Analyze the situation better."

A POLICE CAR AGGRESSIVELY PULLS UP ON THE CURB AND JEREMY TAKES OFF RUNNING.

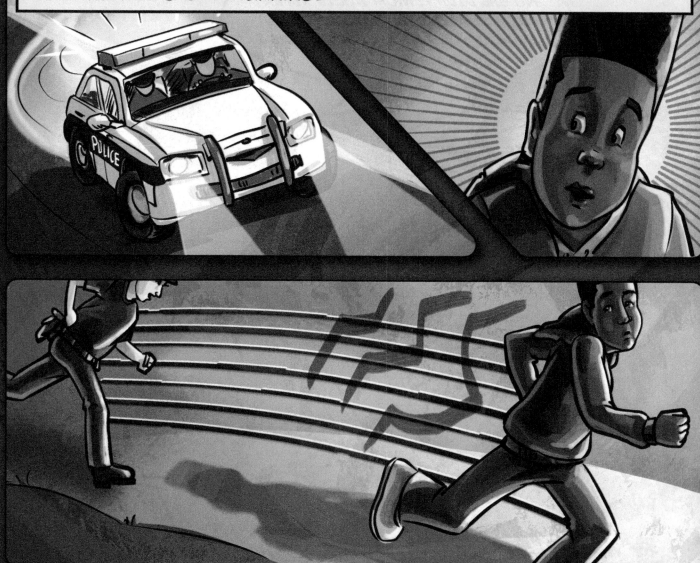

OFFICER MARTINEZ CATCHES UP WITH JEREMY AND TACKLES HIM FROM BEHIND.

I DIDN'T DO ANYTHING. GET OFF OF ME. I CAN'T BREATHE!

 "What are your opinions on the recent officer-involved shootings?"

 "We don't really feel safe around officers and that burns many bridges with them. We don't trust most of them. Are they really out to protect and serve or to annihilate and conquer?"

OFFICER JACOBS SHOOTS RASHAWN FIVE TIMES. JEREMY SCREAMS...

OFFICER JACOBS APPROACHES RASHAWN WITH HIS GUN DRAWN.

HE SHOT ME. ALL I WANTED TO DO WAS SHOW HIM IT WASN'T REAL...

OFFICER JACOBS PICKS UP THE GUN, SEES THE ORANGE TIP, AND REALIZES IT IS A REPLICA.

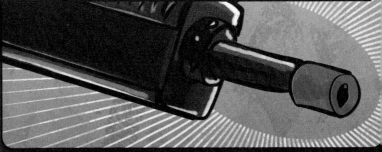

"What is it like to be Black or Hispanic today?"

"I am 6'5", 255 pounds... It's scary for me, I feel like I have to do all I can to make others not fear me. So, that's why I'm always telling you guys, look, hey, scoot off to the side of the street, or make way for other people. I'm always thinking, how can I not make that other person feel like I'm a threat."

"What is it like to be Black or Hispanic today?"

"We feel sad because people are being shot for no reason."

"What are your opinions on the recent officer-involved shootings?"

"It's sad, but it's not really unexpected because police have been killing Black people for so long, so now, nobody can be surprised that people are starting to get mad and resist."

 "What solutions do you think will bridge the divide between communities of color and the criminal justice system?"

 "Here in America, if you're for one thing, then it's perceived that you're against the other. Nowadays, if you're pro-Black Lives Matter, then you're anti-cop. If you're pro-cop, then you're anti-Black Lives Matter. We need to look for a solution where someone can be pro-cop and pro-Black Lives Matter."

LIL' G AND MEMBERS OF THE SAUCE STREET GANG APPROACH HIM.

WHAT'S UP LIL' HOMIE?

JEREMY JOINS LIL' G AND HEADS TO HABIB'S STORE.

 "What is it like to be Black or Hispanic today?"

 "It's hard, violence all around, underestimated, undervalued, and marginalized."

AS THEY WALK AWAY, THE STORE GOES UP IN FLAMES.

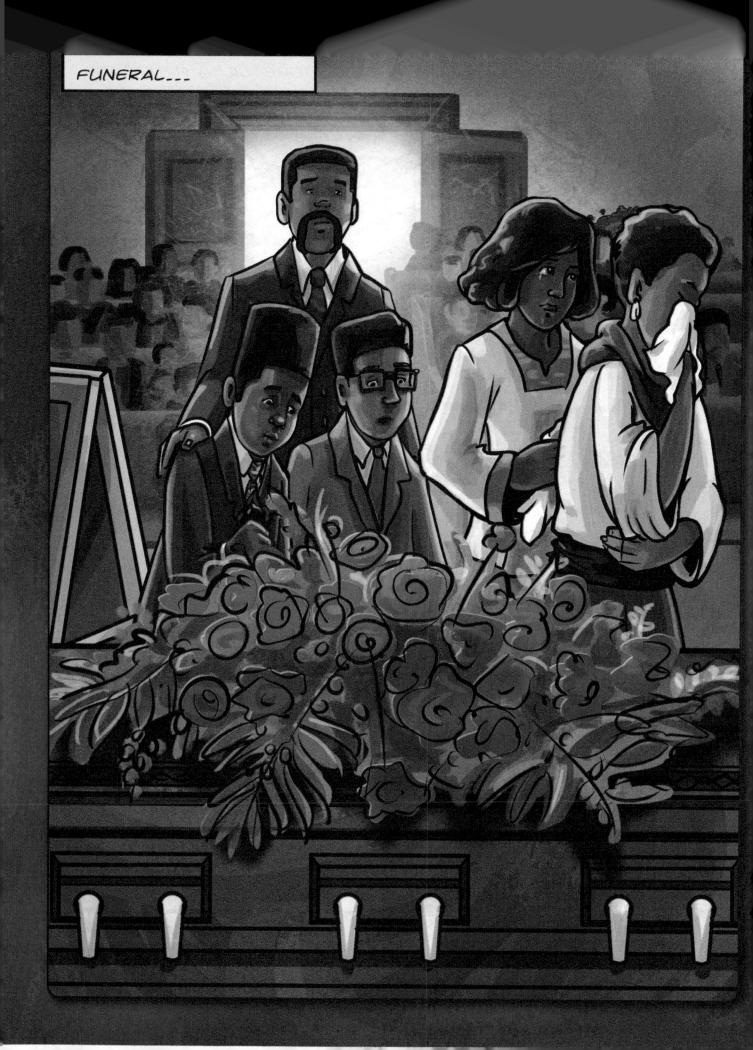

REV. TURNER DELIVERS RASHAWN'S EULOGY.

CHURCH, MY HEART IS HEAVY THIS AFTERNOON. RASHAWN WASHINGTON WAS ONE OF OUR BEST AND BRIGHTEST MEMBERS OF THIS COMMUNITY. I REMEMBER WHEN HE WAS STRUGGLING WITH A MATH CLASS IN THE FIFTH GRADE. I TOLD RASHAWN THAT FOR EVERY "A" HE GETS ON HIS REPORT CARD, I'D GIVE HIM $10. RASHAWN WOULD COME UP TO ME AFTER CHURCH EVERY NINE WEEKS WITH HIS REPORT CARD. HE WOULD GREET ME WITH THIS ENORMOUS SMILE AND SAY, "TIME TO PAY UP, OLD MAN".

TO SISTER MARY, PUT YOUR FAITH IN THE LORD. YOU LOST A SON BUT GOD HAS GAINED ANOTHER ANGEL. RASHAWN LOVED YOU AND HIS BROTHER MORE THAN LIFE ITSELF. TO JEREMY, RASHAWN WOULD WANT YOU TO KNOW THAT IT WASN'T YOUR FAULT. YOUR BROTHER UNEXPECTEDLY BECAME PREY TO A FATE THAT HE TRIED SO DESPERATELY TO PROTECT YOU FROM.

CHURCH, LET'S NOT LET RASHAWN'S DEATH BE IN VAIN. WE MUST NOT REST UNTIL JUSTICE IS SERVED.

AS THE FAMILY LEAVES THE CHURCH, THEY NOTICE A POLICE OFFICER WAITING OUTSIDE.
WHAT'S GOING ON?
JEREMY WASHINGTON, YOU'RE UNDER ARREST FOR ARSON AND DESTRUCTION OF PROPERTY.

"What solutions do you think will bridge the divide between communities of color and the criminal justice system?"

"It's going to take a lot of communication and hearing from both parties on how we can communicate and come to a conclusion that works for everybody, so that everybody feels safe."

"It's a cold world. Where is the love and peace? It seems like life is on repeat. Dude had a toy gun and they still shot him. It seems like what Dr. King fought for doesn't even matter, they still want to see our blood splattered. It seems like if we talk, we get a bullet. It makes me think about what to do in life. Do I need to carry a gun? I go to church and they say something about what they are going to do, but I don't really see them doing anything. People talk a big game about how they are going to stop racism, but when it's time for action, no one is around. Police or people in general assume what other people are going to do with a gun, thinking they're right and we're wrong. The movie Fruitvale Station comes to mind. In the movie, the black dude (Michael B. Jordan who plays Oscar Grant) didn't do anything and got shot. For what reason? If you want something done you have to take a stand and fight. Maybe not physically, but mentally like Dr. King. He fought with words, Rosa sat. There is a difference in fighting for what you believe in and fighting with violence. People make mistakes but don't want to be corrected. It makes me think, are we really free or free to think we're free. We all have two ears, two eyes, one mouth, one nose and red blood. Why are we doing all of this because of color? We are different shades of light. Some lighter, some darker. Black is just a darker shade of light. We all have one brain, we are all bright. Take a stand."

Laurence Jones, 16, Portsmouth, Virginia

ACKNOWLEDGEMENTS

This project would not have been possible without the grace and mercy of the Most High.

To my fiancé Talisha, and daughters Mali and Morgan, thank you for your patience, love and understanding.

To Imagine That! Design, thank you for bringing my stories to life and providing quality service. Special thanks to my editors and contributors, Tiffany Carey Day, Laurence Jones, Francesca Lyn, and Samantha Willis. I'd like to give an extra special thanks to my junior editorial team, Dion Allen, Jamal Ball, Christian Brown, Diojé Ellis, Tiojé Ellis, Ricardo Henson, Terrell Hundley, Tamaje Jones, and Isaiah Taylor.

To my beautiful and supportive family: Ronnie Sidney, Sr., Gwendolyn Sidney, Cherlanda Sidney-Ross, Van Ross, Deandre Sidney, Sydney Ross, Endia Ross, Robert Patrick, Sarah Harris, Etta Wright, Gail Wright, Tony Harris and Gil Holmes.

To some very special individuals and organizations: MP-NNCSB; Chuck Walsh; Emily Eanes; Rachel Teagle; Richmond Association of Black Social Workers (RABSW); Kevin Holder; Renata Hedrington-Jones, PhD; Daryl Fraser; Virginia Commonwealth University (VCU); Nicki Lee, PhD; Mayor Levar Stoney; Understood.org; Virginia Department of Education; Anne Holton; Marianne Moore; Ellen Harrison; Pat Abrams, PhD; Martha Hicks; Essex County Public Schools; Ruth Tobey; Patrick Doyle; Virginia Education Association (VEA); Dr. Antoinette Rogers; Martha Hutzel, Central Rappahannock Regional Library; Meldon Jenkins-Jones, Richmond Public Library; Chris Brown; Karla Redditte (NBC 12); Towanda Darden (EYPC); Ernestine Scott (RPS); Erica Coleman (RPS); Dawn Owens; Alabama First Class Pre-K; Dr. Kimberly Johnson; Essex Public Library; I'm Determined; John McNaught; Kim Stump; Cayden Stump; JMU Male Academy for Academic Achievement Academy; De'Shay Turner; Clovia Lawrence; Julie Bright; Sean Miller; Deanna Lavery; Chad Lewis; Shawn Long; Christopher Pitts; Sean Powell; Derek Hence; Christopher O'Neal; Ebony Campbell; David Miller; Kwame Alexander; Margaret Ransone; Chris Rose (Rappahannock Times); Rich Morgan (WRAR); Kelsee Scott; Rappahannock Community College; Reynolds Community College; Old Dominion University; Good Hope Baptist Church.

To the rest of my family and friends, thank you for your support and words of encouragement throughout this difficult project.

In closing, I wish to dedicate this book to the memory of Michael Brown, William Chapman, Danroy Henry, Jr., Aiyana Jones, Trayvon Martin, Laquan McDonald, and Tamir Rice.

THE WALL OF PRIDE

▲ The James Madison University Male Academy For Academic Achievement Standing With Ronnie Sidney, II, LCSW

▲ A Mother And Son Show Their Support For "Rest In Peace RaShawn" At The African American Cultural Festival Of Raleigh & Wake County

▲ The Norfolk Redevelopment And Housing Authority Invited Ronnie Sidney, II, LCSW To Do An Author Visit At Chesterfield Heights Academy (ES)

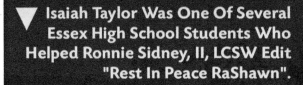

The Westmoreland Children And Youth Association Wrote Essays After Reading The "Rest In Peace RaShawn" Script

The Junior Editorial Team Was Formed At Ronnie Sidney, II, LCSW's Former High School In Tappahannock, Virginia.

Rest In Peace RaShawn Community Forum Participants At Essex High School In Tappahannock Virginia

FLEX YOUR RIGHTS

RULE #1: ALWAYS BE CALM AND COOL.

A BAD ATTITUDE GUARANTEES A BAD OUTCOME. IF YOU KEEP YOUR COOL, CHANCES ARE THE OFFICER WILL TOO.

RULE #2: COPS CAN LIE. DON'T GET TRICKED.

POLICE ARE ALLOWED TO LIE TO YOU. DON'T LET FALSE THREATS OR PROMISES TRICK YOU INTO WAIVING YOUR RIGHTS.

RULE #3: DON'T AGREE TO A SEARCH. EVER.

SAYING "NO" TO SEARCHES IS YOUR CONSTITUTIONAL RIGHT AND PROBABLY YOUR BEST MOVE. COPS MIGHT SEARCH YOU ANYWAY IF YOU REFUSE – BUT YOUR REFUSAL CAN PROTECT YOU LATER IF YOU END UP IN COURT.

RULE #4: DON'T JUST WAIT. ASK: "AM I FREE TO GO?"

ASKING TO LEAVE SHOWS THAT YOU'RE NOT AGREEING TO THE POLICE STOP. THIS CAN PROTECT YOU LATER IF YOU END UP IN COURT.

RULE #5: DON'T DO SHADY STUFF IN PUBLIC.

MAKING DUMB DECISIONS IN PUBLIC IS THE EASIEST WAY TO FIND YOURSELF IN JAIL. ALWAYS THINK BEFORE YOU ACT, ESPECIALLY WHEN OTHER PEOPLE ARE WATCHING.

Special thanks to Steve Silverman, Founder of Flex Your Rights, for providing the information below. Learn more by logging onto FlexYourRights.org.

RULE #6: DON'T ADMIT ANYTHING. REMAIN SILENT.

COPS AREN'T LOOKING FOR AN EXPLANATION; THEY'RE LOOKING FOR EVIDENCE. DON'T GIVE THEM ANY.

RULE #7: ASK FOR A LAWYER.

TRYING TO TALK YOUR WAY OUT OF TROUBLE WITH POLICE IS A BIG MISTAKE. IF YOU'RE BEING INTERROGATED OR YOU'RE UNDER ARREST CALMLY AND CLEARLY STATE, "I'M GOING TO REMAIN SILENT. I WANT A LAWYER." REPEAT IF NECESSARY.

RULE #8: DON'T LET THEM IN WITHOUT A WARRANT.

WITH FEW EXCEPTIONS, POLICE NEED A WARRANT TO ENTER YOUR HOME. UNLESS YOU CALLED FOR HELP, THERE'S GENERALLY NO GOOD REASON TO LET POLICE INTO YOUR HOME.

RULE #9: DON'T PANIC. REPORT MISCONDUCT LATER.

PAY ATTENTION TO DETAIL. WRITE DOWN EVERYTHING YOU SAW AND HEARD. IF YOU PLAN TO SUE OR COMPLAIN, DON'T TELL THE OFFICER.

RULE #10: FILM THE POLICE!

IF YOU WANT TO PROVE POLICE MISCONDUCT, VIDEO EVIDENCE IS THE BEST EVIDENCE. YOU HAVE THE RIGHT TO RECORD THE POLICE IN ALL 50 STATES.

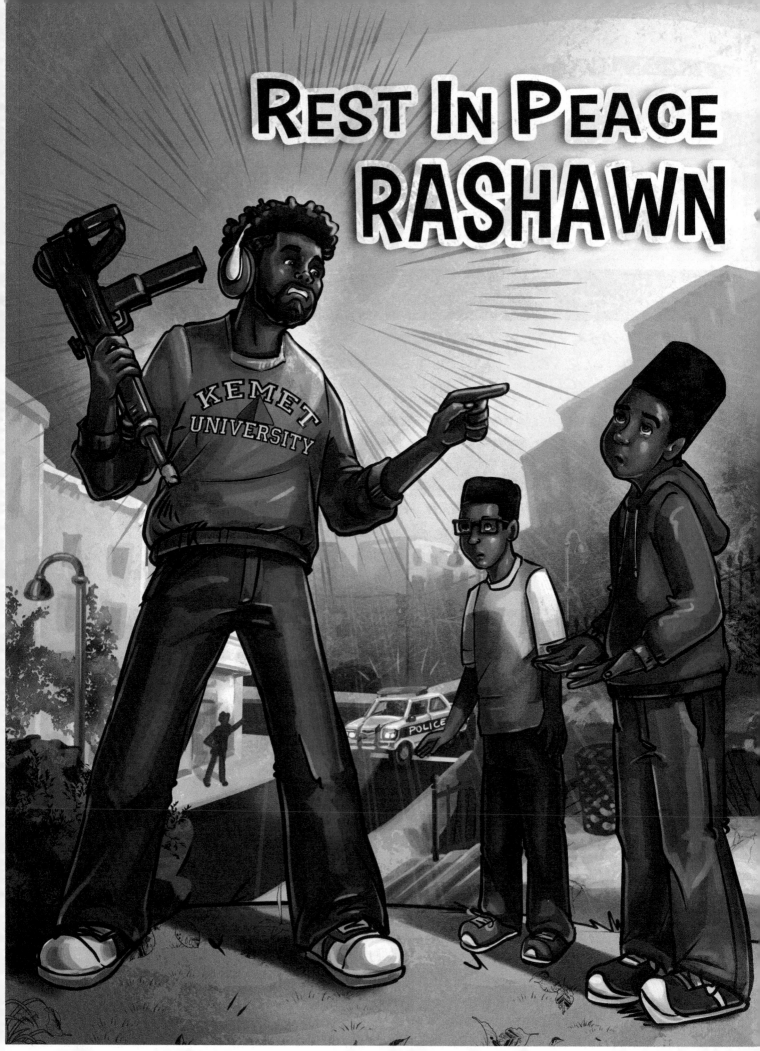

03/18

CPSIA information can be obtained
at www.ICGtesting.com
Printed in the USA
LVOW05s1557050318
568696LV00005B/45/P